McBride

Richard Scarry's
Farmer
Patrick Pig

A Golden Book • New York

Western Publishing Company, Inc., Racine, Wisconsin 53404

Western Publishing offers a wide range of fine juvenile and adult activities, games, and puzzles. For more information write Golden Press, 120 Brighton Road, Dept. M, Clifton, NJ 07012.

Farmer Pig's Busy Day

Patrick Pig was a farmer.
His wife was a farmer, too.
Her name was Penny.
They got up early every morning.

"Here is your breakfast,"
Penny said.
"It is a pickle."
"Good! I love pickles,"
said Patrick.

Farmer Pig put on his straw hat.
Then he went outside. He had
to feed the hens and chicks.
He put the eggs in a basket.

He went to the barn.
He milked the cow.
Oh, no! The cow
knocked over the milk.
What a mess!

Next Patrick got
into his truck.
He went to meet the train.
A box was coming
by train.

In the box was a new hat
for Penny.
Patrick tried it on for fun.
"Look at you!"
said the train man.

When Patrick got home,
he gave the hat to Penny.
"Thank you, my dear," she said.
She gave Patrick a big hug.
Then she gave him a pickle
for lunch.

After lunch Patrick brought
the hay in from the fields.
His cow loved to eat
hay and straw.

Patrick put the hay into the barn.
Oh, no! The wind blew his hat off.

The hat flew up into the barn.
Patrick wanted to get it back.

But first he needed a drink.
So Patrick went
to the well.
Oops! He fell in!

Penny Pig came along.
"What are you doing
down there?" she said.
Then she pulled him out.
But her new hat fell in!

She pulled that out, too.
She put it back on.
And then she and Patrick
went in for supper.
They ate seven pickles.

And Farmer Pig's cow found
Farmer Pig's hat in
Farmer Pig's barn.
And Farmer Pig's cow ate
Farmer Pig's hat for supper.

Farmer Pig's Helper

One morning Patrick Pig
ate breakfast.
"We need someone to help us
on our farm," he said.

Patrick got into his truck.
He drove to town.

He saw someone.

"What is your name?" asked Patrick.

"Thumble," answered the man.

"Would you help us
on our farm?" asked Patrick.
"I would love to,"
said Thumble.

"First you must learn to
drive our truck," said Patrick.
"Drive us back to the farm."

They had to cross a bridge.

"This is not the way
to drive our truck,"
said Patrick.

Luckily Farmer Fox came by.
He pulled them out
of the water.

Thumble drove to the farm.
He went through the gate.
He did not open it first.

Thumble drove through the yard.
He drove through Penny's wash.

"Would you milk our cow?"
asked Patrick.
"I would love to," said Thumble.

Thumble milked the cow.
But then he spilled the milk.

"Would you water our
pickle garden?" asked Patrick.

"I would love to," said Thumble.
Thumble tried to water the garden.
He watered Penny's kitchen instead.

They sat down and had supper.
"Would you clear the table?"
asked Penny.
"I would love to," said Thumble.

Thumble cleared the table.
"You are of no help to us,"
said Patrick.
"We need a helper who can help.
I will drive you back to town."

Patrick drove the truck.
They had to cross a bridge.
Oh, dear!
Patrick really does need
someone who can help!